This igloo book belongs to:

.... Ivy ....

Contents

igloobooks

Published in 2017
by Igloo Books Ltd
Cottage Farm
Sywell
Northants
NN6 0BJ
www.igloobooks.com

LEO002 0517
4 6 8 10 9 7 5 3
ISBN: 978-1-78670-030-8

Printed and manufactured in China
Illustrated by Sophie Hanton
Stories by Elizabeth Dale

5 Minute Tales
Stories for Girls

igloobooks

Dress-Up Magic

Katie was really excited when her mother brought home a fairy wand for her. She loved dressing up. "Thank you!" cried Katie as she waved the wand around. "Do you think it's magic?"

"There's one way to find out," replied her mother. "Why don't you make a wish?" So, Katie waved her magic wand.

"I wish that Jenny would come and play today," she cried.
Suddenly, the doorbell rang. It was Jenny. "Can you play?" she asked.

Katie was amazed. "Yes!" she replied. "Come in and see what I've got!"
Katie twirled her wand. "Mom bought it for me," she said.
"Oh, how lovely!" cried Jenny.
"It's magic," whispered Katie, smiling.

The two friends hurried up to Katie's bedroom. "Do you have any dress-up clothes?" asked Jenny. "I'd love to be a fairy princess."

"No," replied Katie. Then, she smiled. "I wish we could be fairy princesses!" she said, waving her wand.

Suddenly, her mother opened the door. "Look what I found!" she said, holding out two floaty dresses with fairy wings attached.

Jenny and Katie danced around the bedroom. They felt like real fairies. Katie's kitten, Patches, ran around, too. They all danced out into the hallway.

"I am a brave fairy princess," shouted Jenny. "I'm ready to fight the bad pixies in fairyland."

"I wish that pixies would come for Jenny to fight!" cried Katie, waving her wand. Katie and Jenny waited and waited, but no pixies appeared. "My magic's stopped working," sighed Katie.

Katie tried another wish. "I wish that Patches would disappear!" she said, waving her wand again.

Katie and Jenny looked around them. They looked all over, even in the playroom. They couldn't see Patches anywhere. "How clever, Katie!" cried Jenny. "Will your magic wand bring Patches back again."

Katie waved her wand. "I wish that Patches would come back!" she said. Jenny and Katie waited and waited, but Patches didn't return.

"Oh, no!" cried Jenny. "What if Patches never comes back?"
"This is a disaster!" said Katie. "Patches, come back, now!"
"Patches!" called Jenny, but Patches didn't reappear.

Suddenly, they heard footsteps coming up the stairs. Jenny grabbed Katie.
"It's the pixies," she whispered. "You wished they would come and they have!"
"Now I feel really scared. Look, the door knob is turning!"
"Oh, no!" they cried as the bedroom door opened, slowly.

It was only Katie's mother. "Why are you both shouting?" she asked.
"What's the matter?"
"I made Patches disappear with my magic, but I can't make him come back
again," said Katie. "I don't know what to do."

"I'm sure he's around somewhere," said Katie's mother. "Why don't you try
waving your wand again?"

So, Katie waved her wand. "Please come back, Patches," she wished. Suddenly, there was a *meow* from the dress-up box. It was Patches!

"Oh, Patches," said Katie, hugging him. "I'm so glad we found you."
"Was he there all the time?" asked Jenny. "Or did magic make him disappear?"
"I'm not sure," replied Katie. "But I'll only wish for things I really want next time!"

Picture Perfect

Suzy loved painting. She painted pictures of everything around her. So, when she heard that there was going to be a painting competition at the village show, Suzy couldn't wait to enter.

"It says you have to paint a picture of something you love," said Suzy's mother. "Why don't you paint Scruffy?"

Suzy smiled. She thought that was a great idea because she loved Scruffy, her puppy, very much. "Scruffy, where are you?" she called.

Village Painting Competition under 9 years old

Scruffy was digging in the yard. He looked like a mess, covered in mud and leaves.
"You can't paint him like that," said Suzy's mother. "We'll give him a bath."

Giving Scruffy a bath was easier said than done. He splashed about so much that
water went everywhere!

When she had dried off, Suzy started her picture, but Scruffy kept running away. So, Suzy's mother gave him a big, juicy bone. Finally, he was still.

Suzy worked hard and her picture was almost done. She was just about to paint Scruffy's red collar when he jumped up in excitement, to see what she was doing. Scruffy accidentally knocked Suzy's arm and she smudged the red paint.

Suddenly, Scruffy had a red streak right across his face in the picture! It was ruined. "Oh, Scruffy!" cried Suzy.
"Never mind," said her mother. "You've just got time to paint another picture."

Suzy had never painted so fast. Soon she'd finished. She left her picture outside to dry while she went inside to have a drink and some cookies.

Scruffy ran after Suzy, but his paws were covered in paint. "Oh, no!" cried Suzy, running back outside. Suzy couldn't believe her eyes. Scruffy had walked right across her painting. It was covered in doggy paw prints!

"Oh, dear," said her mother "What a naughty dog."
"Woof!" went Scruffy, gazing up at them with his big, brown eyes.

"What am I going to do?!" wailed Suzy. "My painting's ruined. I can't enter the competition now."
"Just take that one to the show," said her mother. "It's still lovely."

Suzy didn't think it was lovely at all. But she really wanted to enter the competition and the show started in five minutes. She had no choice.

When Suzy got to the show, she suddenly worried that she wouldn't be allowed to enter. "This painting is for the Under Nine Year Old Painting Competition," she told the lady. "But it's not all my own work."

"Did your mother help?" asked the lady.

"No," replied Suzy. "My dog did."

"Oh," said the lady, smiling. "Is your dog under nine years old?"

"Yes," replied Suzy.
"In that case you can enter," said the lady.

Suzy smiled with relief. Then, she saw all the other paintings. They were wonderful. "I'm not going to win," she told her mother, sadly.

"Well, you had fun doing your picture, didn't you?" said her mother, hugging her. Suzy smiled. She had, but not as much fun as Scruffy.

Suzy enjoyed looking at the other pictures in the competition.

Then, finally, the results of the painting competition were announced. Suzy clapped as the winner was given a painting set and the person in second place got a box of pencils.

"The third prize, for a painting of her pet, Scruffy, helped by Scruffy, goes to Suzy Price!" said the judge.

Suzy couldn't believe her ears. She and Scruffy had won a prize!
Scruffy wagged his tail, happily, as Suzy took him up to get her prize.
Everyone clapped and cheered.

"Well done!" said the judge, handing Suzy a sketch pad. "Now you can draw lots of pictures of Scruffy."

Suzy smiled. Scruffy was wagging his tail even faster. He clearly thought this was a very good idea, indeed!

The Dancing Fairy

Louise loved staying at her gran's. She got lots of hugs and delicious cakes to eat, as well as fantastic bedtime stories. The only problem was that Louise had no one of her own age to play with.

Every day, she watched the children next door dancing and playing. More than anything, she wished she could join in the fun and be just like them.

The problem was, Louise was very shy and rather clumsy. All her life she'd longed to dance, but every time she tried, she couldn't quite get it right. How could she join in next door if she was going to make a fool of herself?

Louise was so lonely, she stood in front of the mirror and began to cry.

"Are you all right?" asked Gran. She hugged Louise and kissed her.
"No," replied Louise, sobbing, and she told Gran all about wanting to dance.

Gran hugged her tight. "It's about who you are inside that really matters,"
she said, "and you are lovely."
"But I'm still clumsy on the outside," said Louise, sadly.

"I know what will cheer you up," said Gran. "Why don't you go for a walk in the orchard? The trees are so magical and who knows, maybe you'll see some fairies flying around!"

Louise looked at Gran. Did she really believe there were fairies in the orchard? "Oh, well," she said. "I suppose it's better than sitting here doing nothing."

The orchard was beautiful. Delicate pink and white blossoms covered the trees and as Louise walked between them, she began to feel happier. She sat under a tree and closed her eyes.

Suddenly, lovely twinkling music filled the air. Louise opened her eyes. She couldn't believe what she saw. A beautiful fairy was dancing towards her. "Come and join me!" said the fairy.

Louise laughed out loud. "So, fairies do exist!" she cried.
"Yes," replied the fairy, smiling, "and I'm here to help you learn to dance."
She held out her hand. Slowly, Louise got to her feet. "But I can't dance,"
she said, suddenly feeling shy and nervous.

Before she knew it, Louise was whirling and twirling, doing the daintiest steps.
She felt as light as air and not clumsy at all. It was magical!

Louise and the fairy danced through the orchard. Louise waved her arms and pointed her toes. "You can dance," said the fairy. "You can do anything if you believe in yourself."

Soon, it was time for the fairy to go. "Good-bye and thank you," said Louise, as she twirled through the orchard, all by herself.

Gran was waiting for Louise. "Did you meet anyone nice in the orchard?" she asked, winking. Louise laughed and hugged her. Gran knew about the fairy all along. That was why she had sent her outside.

Suddenly, there was the sound of music and laughter next door. "Why don't you go and play?" her Gran asked.

Louise wasn't sure. She still felt shy, but then she remembered what the fairy had told her. "I can dance," she said to herself.

Louise smiled and dashed next door. Everyone was dancing and having fun.
"Come and join us!" cried Emma and Lucy. "We're just making up a new dance.
Would you like to help us make up a routine?"

"I'm not very good," said Louise, and then she twirled and whirled around.
"You dance beautifully!" Emma and Lucy cried.
Louise smiled happily and together they all invented wonderful dances.

Louise danced with the fairy in the orchard each morning and then played with her new friends next door. It was so much fun.

When it was time to go home, Louise said good-bye to Emma and Lucy, then Gran gave her a big hug. "Come back soon," she said. "Come back soon!" echoed a fairy voice from the orchard. "I will," said Louise. "I can't wait and it's all thanks to the dancing fairy!"

The Magic Unicorn

Sarah stared, sadly, at the pony posters stuck all over her bedroom wall.
More than anything in the world she wanted her own pony. The problem was,
Mom didn't have money to buy her one. Her dream would never come true.
"I wish there was some way I could have my own pony," said Sarah, sadly.

Suddenly, Sarah heard a strange noise outside. She looked out of her window and saw a beautiful sparkling unicorn standing under the apple tree.

Sarah ran downstairs to look. She held out her hand and the unicorn softly nuzzled it. She stroked his coat and it was so soft and silky. "I wonder what your name is?" said Sarah. "You've appeared as if by magic. That's it," said Sarah. "I'll call you Magic!"

Sarah climbed onto Magic's back. The unicorn walked forward gracefully, then
he started trotting, then cantering until suddenly, incredibly, he lifted off the ground

Before long they were flying, far above the clouds, to a magical land.

"Wow!" gasped Sarah, as she looked below. "We're in Fairyland!"

There were meadows full of flowers, crystal clear streams, pretty tinkling waterfalls and amazing, musical fountains. Magic flew down and landed gently by a beautiful, pink castle with towers and turrets.

As Sarah jumped off the unicorn's back, fairies flew to greet her. "Welcome to Fairyland!" said one. "I'm Crystal Wing. You're just in time for our party. Do you like parties?"

"Oh yes," replied Sarah, laughing.
"First I'll magic you a party dress!" said Crystal Wing. She waved her wand and suddenly, Sarah was wearing a beautiful party dress.

The party began and all the fairies were there. There were lemonade fountains, delicious sandwiches, yummy cookies, and lots of lovely cupcakes. It was a real fairy feast and Sarah wanted to enjoy every minute of it.

There was a bouncy castle, swings, and a slide. Sarah had a wonderful time eating the party food and Crystal Wing even gave Sarah her very own magic wand!

Soon, the party was over and it was time to leave Fairyland.

Sarah thanked all the fairies and climbed on Magic's back. Before long they were flying up into the sky again. Sarah laughed as they flew into white, fluffy clouds and then swooped down over fields and villages, woods and streams. Finally, they landed back in Sarah's backyard.

Sarah stroked Magic's nose. He neighed softly and nuzzled her hand.
"I've had an amazing time," said Sarah. "Please come back."
Magic nodded his head as if saying, "Yes."

Sure enough, Magic came back to visit Sarah many times. She was so happy.
Sarah had her very own magic pony, and her trip to Fairyland was only the
beginning of her adventures!

Saving Sammy

Joy and Lulu were very excited. They were on vacation near the ocean and couldn't wait to get to the beach. "I'll race you!" cried Joy, as she ran towards the blue water. Joy loved splashing in the waves, but Lulu was a bit scared of them. She preferred to build sandcastles and look in rock pools.

When Joy had finished paddling, she ran up to Lulu. "Come on," she said. "Let's walk along the beach and explore!"

The two friends had fun looking at their footprints and picking up stones and pretty shells. Suddenly, Lulu stopped and pointed. "There's a cave," she said. "I wonder what's inside?"

"Let's find out," replied Joy, walking towards the dark cave mouth.

Suddenly, there was a strange, echoing cry. It was coming from inside the cave.

"Maybe it's a mermaid!" cried Joy. "She was so excited, she ran right into the dark cave where Lulu couldn't see her.

"Be careful!" called Lulu after her. The cave looked quite scary. "Come back, Joy!" she shouted. But there was no answer. Lulu started to worry. What had happened to her friend? "Joy!" she cried again. But there was still no answer.

Feeling scared, Lulu tip-toed slowly into the cave and called again. She heard a cry. It was Joy. "Help!" cried Joy.

Lulu forgot her fear and rushed further into the cave. As her eyes got used to the darkness she could just see Joy. She was kneeling down by a rock. "There's something trapped behind this rock," said Joy.

Lulu grabbed the rock and tried to help Joy push it. But the huge stone wouldn't move. A faint wailing sound came from behind it.

Desperately, Joy and Lulu pushed again. Suddenly, Lulu heard the waves crashing behind them. She turned round, anxiously. "I think the tide's coming in," she said. "What if we get trapped inside this cave?"

"We have to be quick!" replied Joy. "Push!"

The friends both pushed harder than ever. Slowly the rock began to move. Behind it was a baby seal with huge, sad eyes. "Oh, he's so cute," said Joy, stroking the little seal, softly. "Let's call him Sammy!"

The little seal gazed up at them with big, sad eyes. Suddenly, he waddled slowly towards them. "We've saved you, Sammy!" cried Joy.

"Not yet we haven't," cried Lulu. "Look!"
The tide was sweeping into the cave. If they weren't quick, they'd all be trapped.

Joy and Lulu quickly picked up the baby seal and, as the waves lapped around their ankles, carefully carried him out of the cave. Gently, they put Sammy down in the ocean.

Lulu and Joy held their breath as the tiny seal bobbed up and down in the waves. Suddenly, he started swimming and they saw a bigger seal swimming towards him. "That's Sammy's mother!" cried Joy, as the big seal nuzzled her baby. "She's welcoming him back."

Lulu suddenly realized that she was standing in the sea.
"I'm not afraid of the water anymore!" she cried.

Sammy and his mother watched as the two friends laughed
and splashed back to the beach. They made a fantastic sandcastle
of their new friend. Joy and Lulu both agreed it was the best
vacation they had ever had, especially as they spent it saving Sammy!